Fancy NANCY

by Jane O'Connor
pictures by Robin Preiss Glasser

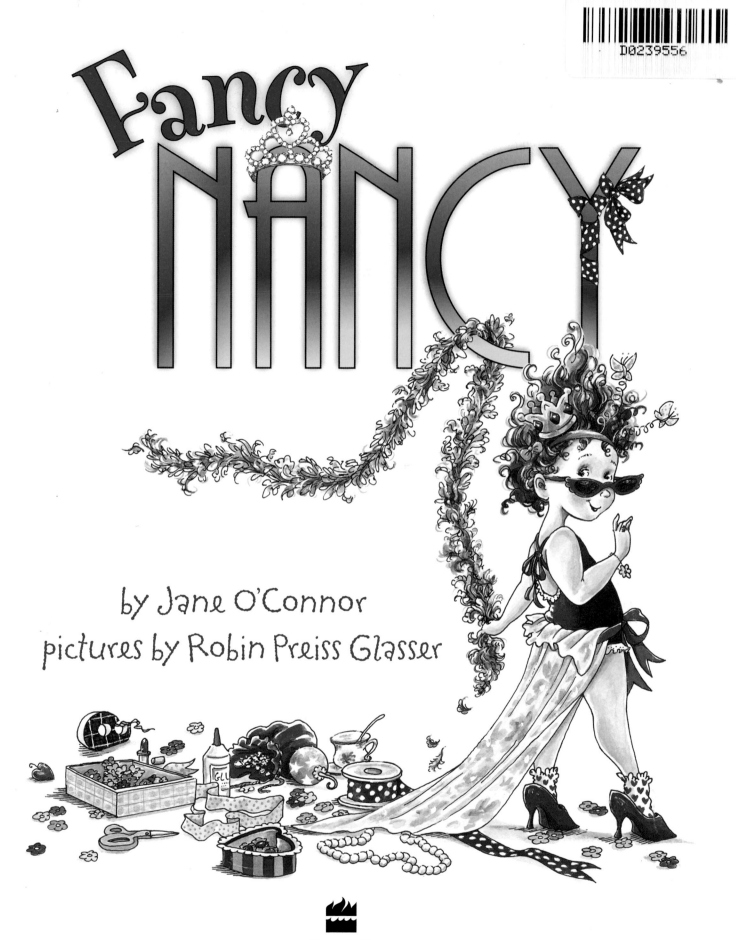

HarperCollins *Children's Books*

For Margaret Frith, pal *extraordinaire*
(that's fancy <u>and</u> French for great)
—J. O'C.

For Jessie, who herself wore
rhinestones to Pre-K
—R.P.G.

This is my room before I made it fancy.

First published in hardback in the U.S.A. by HarperCollins Publishers Inc. in 2006
First published in paperback in Great Britain by HarperCollins Children's Books in 2007

3 5 7 9 10 8 6 4 2

ISBN-13 978-0-00-725346-3
ISBN-10 0-00-725346-X

HarperCollins Children's Books is a division of HarperCollins Publishers Ltd.

Text copyright © Jane O'Connor 2006
Illustrations copyright © Robin Preiss Glasser 2006

The author and illustrator assert the moral right to be identified as the author and illustrator of the work.
A CIP catalogue record for this title is available from the British Library. All rights reserved.
No part of this publication may be reproduced, stored in a retrieval system or transmitted in any form
or by any means, electronic, mechanical, photocopying, recording or otherwise, without the prior permission of
HarperCollins Publishers Ltd, 77–85 Fulham Palace Road, Hammersmith, London W6 8JB.

Typography by Jeanne L. Hogle

Visit our website: www.harpercollinschildrensbooks.co.uk

Printed in China

I love being fancy.

My favourite colour is fuchsia.
That's a fancy way of saying purple.

I like to write my name with a pen that has a plume.
That's a fancy way of saying feather.
And I can't wait to learn French because *everything* in French sounds fancy.

Nobody in my family is fancy at all.
They never even ask for sprinkles.

There's a lot they don't understand...

Lace-trimmed socks *do* help me to play football better.

Sandwiches *definitely* taste better when you stick in frilly toothpicks.

A princess is supposed
to keep her tiara on.

"What's a fancy girl to do?"
I ask my doll, Marabelle.
Her full name is Marabelle
Lavinia Chandelier.

Then I get an idea that is stupendous.
That's a fancy word for great.

Maybe I can teach my family how to be fancy.
I make an advert and stick it on the fridge.

Soon there is a knock on my door.
My family saw the advert. They want to
get started right away.

The trouble is, my family doesn't own any fancy clothes.

That's OK. I go and find – what is that fancy word?
Oh, yes! – some accessories.

Ooo-la-la! My family is posh!
That's a fancy word for fancy.

My mum twirls in front of the mirror.
"Why don't we go somewhere fancy tonight?"

"How about dinner at The King's Crown?" Dad suggests.
Wow! My parents are acting fancier already.

"May I escort you lovely ladies outside?
The limousine is waiting."

My dad is our chauffeur.
That's a fancy word for driver.

When we arrive at The King's Crown,
everyone looks up.
They probably think we're movie stars.

I am so proud of my whole family.
They eat with their pinkies up and
call each other "darling".

Darling!

"For dessert, let's have *parfaits*," my mum says.
"That's French for ice cream sundaes."

Amazing! My mother knows French!

When our parfaits are ready,
I curtsy and say, "*Merci.*"

I carry the tray like a fancy waiter.

Oops! I trip. I slip.

The tray does a double flip!

I don't feel fancy anymore.

I want to go home.

After I get all cleaned up, I put on my peignoir.
That's a fancy French word for dressing gown.
I feel much better. I'm ready for a parfait.

I tell my parents, "Thank you for being fancy tonight."

"I love you," my dad says.
"I love you," my mum says.

And all I say back is, "I love you."
Because there isn't a fancy – or better – way of saying that.